EMMA
IS ON THE AIR
#3: SHOWTIME!

by IDA SIEGAL

illustrations by
KARLA PEÑA

SCHOLASTIC INC.

Text copyright © 2015 by Ida Siegal
Illustrations copyright © 2015 by Scholastic Inc.

This book is being published simultaneously in hardcover by Scholastic Press.

ISBN 978-0-545-68702-7

10 9 8 7 6 5 4 3   17 18 19 20

Printed in the U.S.A.   40

First printing 2016

Book design by Mary Claire Cruz

CONTENTS

CHAPTER ONE

Dance Class

THIS is the coolest thing ever!" Javier yelled with excitement.

I sat down next to him on the floor of his living room and nodded in agreement. It *was* cool.

"Magnifying glass—check. Binoculars—check." Javier pointed to each of the tools that came in his brand-new spy kit.

"Walkie-talkies—check. Night-vision goggles—check. It's all here! This. Is. Awesome."

I know what you're thinking. We lost the costume contest at the Halloween Festival—so how did Javier get a spy kit? His parents got it for him! Javier's parents told all of us that they were proud of him for doing something *constructive*. Like being part of our reporting team and working hard to solve cases. So they decided to buy him the spy kit as a reward!

"Hey, look," Sophia said, pointing, "it also has a flashlight and a detective badge."

"And it's going to help us solve even more mysteries!" I added.

"Thanks, guys," Javier said as he put the night-vision goggles on his head.

"I don't get it. What's so great about a spy kit?" asked Shakira. She was with us at Javier's house because afterward we were going to walk to our dance class together.

"Spy kits are awesome," Javier answered. "There's so much you can do. Look, these are the night-vision goggles. Watch this." Javier turned off the lights in his living room.

"Hey!" his mother yelled from the hallway. "Who turned out the lights?"

"Whoa." Javier chuckled as he looked around the room. "I can see everything. I can even read what's on the chalkboard in the kitchen! This is awesome."

Then the lights came back on. Javier's mother took the glasses off and lightly bonked him on the head with them.

"No night vision in the living room, please. The rest of us can trip and fall."

"Sorry, Mom," Javier answered. But he was still smiling as his mom went back to the kitchen.

"Look, Emma," Shakira said as she stepped over Javier's spy kit. "I found this headband for you. It has a purple flower on top. It'll go great with your green blazer. Stop playing with your curls and try it on."

Shakira isn't really interested in spy stuff. She would much rather collect jewelry, work on different hairstyles, and put on lip gloss. In fact, Shakira has been helping me figure out news reporter hairstyles. Especially ones that make sure my curls don't fall in my face when I'm trying to explain a story on my show, "Emma Is On the Air."

And it's true: I was playing with my pudding Slinky curls. I like to pull them and watch them spring back up. Especially when I'm thinking about stuff.

I pulled the last curl all the way down, as far as I could. And then I let go and watched it bounce up to my head. Ha! I have the bounciest curls!

"Thanks, Shakira!" I said as I took the headband from her.

"You can use my new mirror," Shakira offered. She had just gotten a new vanity kit for her birthday. Every time you open the mirror, it plays music and a silly voice goes, "You look faaabulous!"

Shakira loves stuff like that. Her new vanity kit is full of hair ties and makeup and lip gloss, too. My mom says I'm not allowed to wear makeup yet. At first I was mad about it, but to be honest, I got over it. I like solving mysteries much more than wearing makeup, anyway.

"Shakira, I really like this headband," I told her. "Thanks!"

"No problem. You look faaabulous," she replied, sounding just like the singing mirror. We all laughed as Javier's mom walked back into the living room.

"Emma, your mom is here to walk you girls to dance class," she told us.

"Okay, thanks," I answered.

"See you later, Javier," Sophia said. But Javier was so busy playing with his spy kit he just nodded and mumbled a quick good-bye.

We are learning a special kind of dance in

our class. It's from the Dominican Republic, and it's called the mangulina.

The best part of the mangulina dance is that all of us girls get to wear big, beautiful dresses! They have really long, flowy skirts that are red, white, and blue. Sophia, Shakira, and I changed into our mangulina skirts as soon as we got to the dance studio.

"Okay, girls, I want you to spin around and move your hips so we can see your colorful skirts twirl in the air!" said Maestra Soto after we began our class. She's our dance teacher. *Maestra* is how you say "teacher" in Spanish. You say it like this: *"my-es-tra."*

"Pick up the sides of your skirts with your hands. Now twirl and hold your skirt up as high as you can!"

Maestra picked up a tambora drum—that's a special drum they use in the Dominican Republic. She started playing the drum while we danced. I spun around and around with every drum beat. When I spin in my mangulina dress, my skirt flies up around me. I can see all the colors blend together. It makes me feel like I'm flying in a rainbow!

"Okay, class . . . everyone gather around," instructed Maestra Soto. We stopped spinning to pay attention. "We're going to take a break from dancing. I want you to have a seat on the floor."

Maestra's son, David, wheeled in a television set on a cart. He's sixteen years old and helps his mom out sometimes.

"We are going to watch the news," Maestra announced.

The news? We all looked at one another, confused. David turned on the TV, and a news reporter came on. She was doing a news report on dancers.

"With grace and beauty, these dancers perform what's traditionally known as the Japanese flower hat dance," the reporter said. "They are one of two local dance groups picked to perform in the Thanksgiving Day Parade this year."

The reporter explained all about the Japanese folk dancers. When the report was over, Maestra Soto turned the TV off.

"Okay, dancers. Do you know why I showed you this news report?" she asked.

"No . . ." we answered all together.

"Because that reporter, Rachel Cheng, is coming here next week to do a news story on *our* dance group, Las Palomas."

We all screamed with excitement.

"Are we gonna be on TV? On the *news*?" Shakira blurted out.

"Yes, you are," Maestra Soto answered.

We squealed again.

"And do you know why we're going to be on the news?" she asked.

We all shook our heads.

"Because Las Palomas—our dance group—has also been asked to perform at the Thanksgiving Day Parade."

That was it. We all got up and started jumping and screaming and dancing in place. This news was just too exciting—we couldn't sit still!

CHAPTER
TWO

Palomas in a Parade

OKAY, boys and girls," said Maestra Soto as she tried to calm us down. "Settle down, everyone. We don't have much time. We have been given an extraordinary opportunity. Another dance group had to drop out of the parade at the last minute. The parade organizers called me and asked if Las Palomas could take their place.

"What do you think I said to that?"

"Yes!" we all screamed.

"You're right—I said yes." Maestra smiled, then looked very serious. "But guess what? The parade is in three weeks. Usually we would have months to prepare. But we have just three short little weeks. Do you think we can do it?"

"Yes!" we all screamed again.

"This means we have to work extra hard to make our routine as close to perfect as possible. I need to see all of you at rehearsals four days a week until the parade. Including Saturdays. This will be a big commitment, but I have confidence we can do it. Don't you, Alyssa?"

Alyssa is Maestra's fourteen-year-old niece. She's a really good mangulina dancer and helps teach the class.

"I think they can do it . . . if they're willing to put in the hard work," Alyssa replied, smiling at us.

"I agree," said Maestra. "Next week that news reporter you just saw, Rachel Cheng, is going to come here and do the story about us. We have to be on our best behavior and get our steps down."

"We will!" I shouted.

"That's what I like to hear," answered Maestra.

Maestra started explaining our rehearsal schedule while Alyssa cleaned up the dance studio. I knew for sure we would be willing to work hard, especially if it meant being in a real news story *and* being in a parade!

I work super hard on my news show, "Emma Is On the Air," all the time. Like when Javier found a worm in his hamburger in the school cafeteria, it took a lot of work to figure out how it got there. But I did it! And after I did my news report on it, the health inspector agreed it was just an accident and no one at our school had to get fired.

And when Sophia lost her Halloween costume, I had to think really, really hard about what to do. But when we worked together, Sophia, Javier, and I found the costume just in time! We even helped our class win a pizza party!

Sophia, Javier, and I have officially become the best mystery-solving and news-reporting team at P.S. 387. Everyone knows we can solve any mystery there is . . . and that's why we're famous!

"Right, Emma? Emma?" Maestra Soto called. I wasn't listening because I was thinking about how famous we were.

"Um, sorry, Maestra. Can you repeat that, please?"

"What I said was, I need everyone to take

home these permission slips after class today and get your parents to sign them so you can be on the news and in the parade."

I nodded and took my permission slip.

"Okay, class. That's it for today. We'll see you all next Tuesday. Alyssa, can you take the tambora drum and lock it in the closet for me, *por favor*?" Maestra asked.

Maestra has told us all about this tambora drum before. It's a very special drum, handmade by her grandfather in the Dominican Republic. Her *abuelo*.

"I'll take good care of it," Alyssa promised. She took the drum just as the rest of us all rushed out of class. I had so much to tell my mom and Papi when I got home!

*   *   *

"So can I, can I, Papi? Please, Mom? Will you sign the permission slip, please?" I asked at dinner that night.

"Of course," Papi replied.

"This sounds wonderful," Mom agreed.

"But remember," said Papi, "you'll be doing a lot of rehearsing, so you may have to give your news show a break for a little while. You can't do everything at once. Will you be okay with that?"

"That's fine!" I shouted.

My cat, Luna, jumped on my lap when she heard the commotion. Baby Mia squealed with delight. She loves it when Luna sits at the table with us. Even though Mom and Papi don't love it so much.

"Sorry, Luna," I told her, "they won't let cats perform at the Thanksgiving Day Parade. Even special cats who are also reporter assistants."

Luna meowed and jumped off my lap and onto her favorite sofa cushion. I asked to be excused from the table. Luna and I raced to my room. I had to practice my magulina moves!

CHAPTER
THREE

The Real News!

THAT week was very busy. I was going to dance rehearsals every other day after school. I was so tired, but rehearsals were going really well. Maestra Soto said she was proud of us ... but we were missing something: boys. Maestra said we needed more boys to join our dance group for the parade performance. I told her I knew the perfect boy for the job!

"Um ... Emma, I'm really not a very good

dancer," Javier said nervously on his first day of rehearsal.

"But, Javier, we took mangulina class together in first grade. Remember? You know how to do it."

"Yeah, but, Emma, that was two years ago. I did it because my mom made me. Why do you think I stopped? I was terrible!"

"Oh, I don't believe that. You'll be great!" I told him.

Javier agreed to join our dance group, but I had to promise him two of my cookies at lunch every day for two weeks. And since he has allergies, I had to make my mom give me the gluten-free kind. I told Javier they taste funny and he said, they do not. And I said, they do, too. And he said, how would you know if you haven't even tried them? And I said, fine, I'll try them! And actually . . . they were pretty good!

Anyway, watching Javier dance was a little funny. Sophia agreed to be his partner, but I think she might regret it. When Maestra said spin to the right, he went left. When Maestra told the boys to grab the girls' hands, he pulled too hard and Sophia landed on his feet! And when Maestra told the boys to kick their feet, Javier stepped on Sophia's skirt by accident and they both fell to the ground!

Maestra's son, David, stepped in to help.

"That's it, Javier," David instructed. "Use your right foot next time . . . and then spin."

Eventually Javier got better. We all did. We rehearsed so much, my arms felt like Jell-O. And my legs felt wobbly when I walked home from class. But our dance performance was looking great! Shakira and Sophia and I were spinning and stepping and shaking at all the right times.

We held our skirts high in the air as we spun around and around.

The following week, we had a very special visitor at dance class.

"Okay, boys and girls," Maestra said with a big smile. "I want to introduce you to someone. This is Rachel Cheng, from the local news station. She is here to do the news story on Las Palomas dance group!"

We all let out a huge giggle as we said hello. I couldn't believe there was a real, famous reporter right in front of me. She was holding a real microphone and there was a man with a real camera standing next to her. It was so cool.

"I want you to be on your best behavior and cooperate with Ms. Cheng, okay?" said Maestra.

"Okay," we all replied.

"Who can tell Ms. Cheng why we are called Las Palomas?"

"Ooh, me! I can, I can!" I shouted.

"Wow, you seem to know the answer," Rachel Cheng said, smiling right at me. "But please, call me Rachel. And this guy here is my video photographer, Christian." We waved hi to Christian, too. "So," Rachel continued, "I'd love to know what Las Palomas means." Then she looked at Christian and motioned to me. He lifted his huge video camera and pointed it right at me! Then Rachel picked up her microphone and pointed that at me as well!

I wanted to tell her that I was a reporter, too. That I have a microphone almost the same as hers! I was so excited to talk to a real reporter, for a minute I forgot what I was going to say. I took a deep breath. And then I remembered.

"Las Palomas means 'the Doves,'" I told her. "We are called the Doves because they represent peace and beauty and grace. And so do we."

"Wow. I'm very impressed," said Rachel. I thought for a moment, *Maybe she likes me!* "Thank you for that explanation. I would love to see your dance routine. Can you all perform it for us?"

"Yes!" we shouted back.

"Everyone get into position," Maestra instructed. "Alyssa, can you go get the tambora drum from the closet? I want to play it for this performance. Thanks."

"Sure thing," Alyssa replied. She ran to the corner of the dance studio to open the closet. When Alyssa came back a few seconds later, she didn't have the drum with her.

"Sorry, I forgot I put it in the closet upstairs yesterday. I'll go get it," Alyssa explained. Maestra and David looked at her strangely.

"Okay, while Alyssa goes to get the drum, we will get started. We'll play the music from my phone instead."

Alyssa ran out of the room, and we got into position. As soon as the music started, we knew what to do. We knew all the right moves and made our skirts fly extra high just to impress the reporter. Even Javier managed not to fall down.

As we were dancing, I saw Alyssa come back into the room. She whispered something to Maestra Soto. Maestra put her hand over her mouth. She looked shocked and worried. Then they both left the room. Shakira and I looked at each other. We didn't know what was wrong, so we kept dancing until our routine was finished.

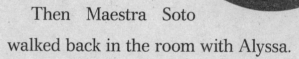

"That was wonderful! Thank you so much for showing that to us," Rachel said.

Then Maestra Soto walked back in the room with Alyssa.

"You've done a great job with these kids, Maestra. They're all so talented," Rachel said. "I think we're almost done shooting our story. But I would like to see that special tambora drum before we leave. Can we get some shots of you playing the drum?"

"Um . . . well . . ." Maestra Soto was stuttering. I knew something was wrong. She usually knows exactly what to say. I looked over at Alyssa, and she looked like she was going to be sick!

"Actually, Rachel," explained Maestra Soto, "it appears as though the tambora drum is . . . missing."

CHAPTER FOUR

Tambora—Taken!

THE drum is missing?" Rachel asked.

"It's all my fault!" Alyssa blurted out. She started crying. "I put it in the closet upstairs and someone stole it!"

"Well, that doesn't sound like your fault," said Rachel. But Alyssa kept crying.

"It's such a special drum," Alyssa said through her tears. "It was handmade in the Dominican Republic! It makes the most beautiful music, and we need it for the parade! Oh, I'm so sorry, Tía.

I didn't mean to," Alyssa cried. She calls Maestra Soto *tía* because that means "aunt" in Spanish.

"It's okay," Maestra told her. "It's not your fault. I know we'll find it."

"I'm so sorry to hear this," Rachel said.

"The truth is," Maestra explained, "that drum does create a beautiful sound. The parade organizers told me it is part of the reason why we were chosen to perform. Without it, I'm afraid we may not be able to do our dance routine the way they wanted it."

Shakira and Sophia and I looked at one another with fear. Did this mean we might not get to be in the parade?

"Oh, no," said Rachel. "That would be awful. And you all have worked so hard—you are such a wonderful addition to this year's parade. Hmm. Maybe I can help . . ."

"Help? Really? But how?" asked Alyssa. Her eyes were red and puffy from crying.

"I'm going to talk about the missing tambora drum in my news report. Can you show me a picture of it?"

"Sure!" said Maestra, perking up. "David, honey, pass me my phone, please." He did, and Maestra showed Rachel a picture of the drum on her phone.

"My grandfather, my *abuelo*, was a drum maker in the town of San Pedro," Maestra explained. "He worked on this tambora so long and hard, everyone said it made the most beautiful music. More beautiful than any tambora they'd ever heard. Look here, see, it's dark brown, with tan ropes on the side and a tan rawhide skin on top where you hit it. It also has a special flower painted on the side with the

Dominican flag. My grandfather said that was for good luck."

"It's beautiful," Rachel said. "I'm going to show this picture on the news. Hopefully someone recognizes it and can tell us where it is."

"That would be wonderful!" said Maestra.

I was so excited to hear that a real reporter would try to help us find the tambora. But still, I thought, we needed to do more than just show the picture on TV. I looked at Shakira, Sophia, and Javier.

"We have to get that tambora back," I said quietly.

"Yeah," said Sophia. "I think that reporter is going to need some help. And I think we can help her!"

"You mean with 'Emma Is On the Air'?" Shakira asked.

"Yup, yup!" I answered with a smile.

"Let's start now!" Javier said.

Javier was right. We had to start right away. So I took off. "Ms. Cheng . . . Ms. Cheng . . ." I called as I ran over to her on the other side of the studio.

"Hi there. Emma, right? You can call me Rachel," she answered.

"Okay. Rachel, can I tell you something?"

"Of course. What is it?"

"Well, I'm so glad that you're going to help us find the tambora," I told her. "We've worked so hard to be in the parade, and we'd be so disappointed if our performance was canceled."

"Of course. I understand. I hope we're able to find the drum for you."

"That's the thing," I went on. "I was thinking

maybe I could help? Rachel, I'm actually a reporter, too. I have my own news show."

"Is that right?" Rachel sounded like she was impressed. "That's fantastic. I'd love to see it sometime."

"Yeah, I'm actually pretty famous. I solve cases at school, and I help people all the time. The truth is, I'm actually *very* famous."

"I see," Rachel said with a chuckle. Although I wasn't sure what was so funny. She saw the confused look on my face and said, "Yes, I can see how that would make you famous. Emma, I can use all the help I can get. Here's my business card." She handed me a small white card that had her name, phone number, and email address on it. "Call me or email me if you figure anything out. We need to work together to find this drum."

"I will! Thanks!"

Rachel walked back over to Maestra Soto and shook her hand before she and Christian the video photographer left.

I ran to tell the guys we were officially on the case. Luckily, I had my camera phone and microphone already in my backpack, ready to go. Even though I hadn't worked on my show in a while, I always kept my reporter equipment in my bag. You never know when a reporting emergency will pop up!

"Okay, guys, step one," I said to Sophia, Javier, and Shakira. "We need to interview witnesses! Who should we interview first?"

"Ooh, I know!" said Shakira. "We should interview Alyssa, right? She's the one who lost the drum."

"Yup! Nice answer, Shakira. First we talk to Alyssa," I agreed. "Shakira, I'm glad you're helping with this investigation. We could use another member of our news team."

"Thanks, Emma," Shakira answered. She looked proud. "Come on, let's go talk to Alyssa before she leaves." Off we went—as a team of four.

CHAPTER
FIVE

Back On the Air

WE found Alyssa on the other side of the dance studio. She was sitting on the floor hugging her knees. She looked really upset.

The four of us approached Alyssa. Sophia was holding the camera. I let Shakira hold the Emma microphone because she never got to before. And Javier was standing next to us taking notes. Well, he was taking notes in his head. He says he doesn't like to write stuff down. So I pulled out my purple reporter pad and shiny

feather pencil. I figured someone should write everything down!

"Hi, Alyssa," I said to her in a gentle voice. "I know you're really upset. But don't worry, we're gonna find the drum. I'm going to help Rachel the reporter with the news story. Can I ask you some questions?"

"Sure. I guess. But, Emma, the drum is gone.

There's no way we'll be able to get it back," Alyssa replied.

"We can at least try," I said. "You said you didn't lock the drum in our closet here in the downstairs studio, right? You locked it in the closet in the upstairs studio?"

"Um . . . yeah." Alyssa took a deep breath. "I usually lock it in our studio closet downstairs, but it was full yesterday. There were too many costumes in there. So I took it upstairs. I found a closet that had enough space. I put the drum inside and locked the door. When I went back today to find it, the drum wasn't there."

"So the upstairs closet was empty?" Javier chimed in. He was holding one finger to his forehead as if he was taking notes in his brain.

"Well, it wasn't empty. It still had other stuff inside," Alyssa said.

"What stuff?" asked Sophia from behind the camera.

"Um, I think there was a pair of dance shoes, a couple CDs, and a duffel bag," Alyssa replied.

"Hmm. Okay, thanks," I said.

Javier, Shakira, Sophia, and I walked back over to the side of the dance studio where we left our coats and bags.

"I know it's time to go home, guys, but before we go, we just have to go to the—"

"Upstairs closet?" Shakira said, cutting me off. She was getting the hang of this.

"That's right!" I said, smiling at her. "Come on, let's go."

We all headed to the upstairs dance studio to inspect the closet. We found it in the far left corner. It was small and looked more like a locker. An old wooden locker. I pulled on the

closet door—and it was open. The lock looked broken. That seemed strange.

"Look," said Shakira. "There are the dance shoes, CDs, and the duffel bag. They're crammed inside. Just like Alyssa said."

"But there's definitely no drum here," added Javier, who had stuck his head inside the closet. He was right: The drum wasn't there. It couldn't be in the duffel bag. It was way too small for the tambora to fit inside.

"This seems funny, though," said Sophia. "It looks like the lock is broken. How could Alyssa have locked the drum here if the lock didn't work?"

"Good question, Sophia," I said.

One of my chocolate pudding Slinky curls had fallen from behind my headband and into my face again. I started playing with it as I always do. I twirled that one loose curl around my finger, and then I pulled it all the way down past my waist. I let go and it sprang back up. Just like a Slinky. But this time, something funny happened. As soon as my curl sprang back up to my head, an idea popped right into my brain!

"Hey, guys, I think we need to check *inside* the duffel bag," I told them.

"Okay, but why?" asked Sophia.

"Yeah, why?" add Javier. "The drum is obviously not in there. That bag is way too small."

"I know," I replied, "I just want to be sure we're not missing anything."

Javier unzipped the bag. It was silver and shiny. We looked inside and saw two dozen paper fans with all kinds of flowers painted on them. It looked like they were used in an old dance routine.

"Aha!" I said.

"What??" Shakira and Javier and Sophia all wanted to know.

"Look at these fans. They're made of paper. But do they look damaged to you?"

"No," said Javier.

"Then we know the drum couldn't have been here," I told them.

"How do we know that?" asked Shakira.

"Look how small the closet is," I answered. "In order to fit a drum in here, you'd have to place it on top of the duffel bag and crush the fans. These fans look just fine to me."

"Oh, wow! You're right!" Sophia said, excited. "These fans are in good condition. There's no way the drum was here." She pressed record on the camera phone and started shooting video of the closet and the un-crushed fans. Just then, a girl from the upstairs ballet class walked in the studio. It looked like she had come back inside to grab her sweatshirt. I thought I knew her from school. A fifth grader.

"Hi!" I said to her.

"Hi," she said back.

"You're Gabriella, right? Do you take ballet up here after school?" I asked.

"Um . . . yeah?" She sounded confused why I was asking.

"I'm Emma. I just wanted to ask you something really quick for my news show. It's called an interview."

"Oh! I know about your show!" she said. "Sure, what's up?"

Sophia pointed the camera in her direction and Shakira held the mic just under her mouth.

"Did you leave right after ballet class yesterday?" I asked Gabriella.

"Actually, I did. But then I had to come back right away because I forgot my sweatshirt," she explained, pointing at a sweatshirt draped over a nearby chair. She grabbed it and looked down at her shoes. "I forget things a lot," Gabriella added, looking embarrassed.

"That's great!" I said.

"My mom doesn't think it's great . . ." she muttered.

"No, no," I said quickly. "I meant it's great for me! You might be able to help with my investigation. What I need to know is, did you see our dance assistant, Alyssa, up here yesterday? She said she was here putting our drum in that closet over there."

"Hmm. I didn't see her," answered Gabriella. "I don't think she came upstairs. I was here for a while, looking for my sweatshirt. Then my mom came up to help me. We didn't see anyone."

"That's what I suspected," I said.

"Oh, and that closet is broken," said Gabriella. "The lock doesn't work. No one uses it. The stuff in there has been sitting there like that for months."

"That's what we thought!" Shakira shouted suddenly. We all giggled a little. "Oops. Sorry, Emma. Keep going."

"Shakira's right. It looked like the lock was broken. Thanks, Gabriella! Nice meeting you."

"No problem. Can't wait to see your news show, Emma. I'm a fan!"

Wow! A fifth grader was a fan of my show! I wanted to smile and laugh, but instead I pretended like it was no big deal. It was more professional that way.

"Thanks, Gabriella. See you at school."

I pulled out my purple reporter pad and my shiny feather pencil. I found the first empty page and wrote The Case of the Missing Tambora. Then underneath I wrote,

Clue #1: The closet in the upstairs studio has a broken lock.

Clue #2: The paper fans were not crushed.

Clue #3: Gabriella says Alyssa wasn't in the upstairs studio after dance

class. The drum couldn't have
been in the upstairs studio closet.

"But, Emma, what does it all mean?" asked Javier. "Was Alyssa lying?"

"Why would Alyssa lie?" asked Shakira.

"I don't know if she was lying or not," I said. "But I do know that her story doesn't make sense. That tambora drum was never here."

CHAPTER
SIX

"Can I? Pleeaase?"

ONCE I got home from dance class, I headed straight for my room. I wanted to get started on my news report right away. But first I had to grab my green velvet blazer with elbow patches and my white pearl necklace. Then I hooked my camera phone up to the computer so I could transfer all the interviews and video we shot at dance class today.

Once everything was ready to go, I wrote my script, arranged my pudding Slinky curls so they weren't falling in my face, and pressed record.

"Hello, everyone! This is Emma and I'm on the air!" I said, staring straight into the camera on my laptop. I told the viewers all about the missing tambora drum. I told them we might not be able to perform in the Thanksgiving Day Parade without it. Then I played the interviews with Alyssa and Gabriella and showed them video of the broken lock and the un-crushed paper fans.

"The investigation continues tomorrow," I said into the camera. "In the meantime, there is a special treat on the real news tonight! A real news reporter named Rachel Cheng is doing a story on our dance group, Las Palomas. In fact, Rachel and I are working together to find the tambora drum! Her report will be on tonight! I hope you like it. That's all for now. I'll see you next time on 'Emma Is On the Air'!"

I posted my report on the school website bulletin board and headed downstairs for dinner. We had my favorite Dominican meal: roasted chicken, white rice, red beans, and—best of all—*tostones*! *Tostones* are like Dominican french fries, but they're not made of potatoes; they're made with plantains. You say it like this: *"toe-stone-es."* Yum!

When we were done eating, Papi said, "Okay, Emma, it's time. Put your plate in the sink and head to the living room."

I zipped through the kitchen and ran to the couch. The news was on, and Rachel's story about my dance class was about to begin!

"Here I am!" I said, panting as I leapt onto the sofa. Mom was holding baby Mia and sitting next to Papi.

"Careful," Mom said, but she was giggling.

"Sorry," I said with a smile.

I could tell she was excited, too. This was the first time I was gonna be on real TV! Papi was playing with the remote to make sure we were recording the news. Just as he hit record, Rachel came on.

"There is no shortage of color and flair when this group of boys and girls are performing," she said, talking into her official reporter's microphone. "This is called the mangulina dance. It is a traditional folk dance from the Dominican Republic, and this group is called Las Palomas."

Then I saw myself on TV, explaining what Las Palomas means! I squeezed Papi's arm and started giggling. It was so funny seeing myself on real TV!

When the part with all of us dancing was over, Mom and Papi looked over at me proudly.

"That was wonderful, honey!" Mom said with excitement.

"*¡Esa es mi niña!*" Papi said. "That's my girl!"

"Hold on," I told them. "The story's not over yet and there's an important part coming up."

Rachel showed the picture of the missing drum.

"Las Palomas desperately needs this drum,"

she said into the camera. "So if any of you have seen it, please reach out to us as soon as possible so we can get it back to them."

"See, I told you guys. We're in big trouble." I'd told Mom and Papi all about the missing drum at dinner.

"That does seem serious," Mom said.

"Papi, I know you said I shouldn't work on 'Emma Is On the Air' while doing the mangulina rehearsals . . . but Rachel said we could work together on this case! And it's so important. Look, she even gave me her business card! Can I, Papi? Can I? Please?"

"Hmm . . ." Papi said. "I've met Rachel Cheng before. She's a very good reporter. I'll reach out to her in the morning to see if they found anything yet."

"Thank you, Papi!" Papi grabbed her business

card from me. "Does that mean I can continue my investigation?"

"*Continue* your investigation?" Papi asked with one eye brow raised.

Oops! I hadn't exactly told Papi that I'd already started the case.

"Um . . . well . . ." I stammered. "I kind of already got started. But we had to! We have to find this drum right away!"

"Okay, okay, *mija*. I understand. Next time, ask first. Okay?"

"Okay!" I agreed.

Thank goodness Papi said yes.

"Emma Is On the Air" is back, baby! I heard that on a pizza commercial once. They said, "Pineapple pizza crust is back, baby!" Now we're back, too! And we're better than pineapple pizza crust. Ew—that sounds super gross. Ha!

CHAPTER SEVEN

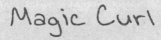

Magic Curl

THE next day at school everyone was talking about Las Palomas. Now that we were on the real news, we were even more famous than before! Even Melissa G. saw us on TV.

"You were . . . okay. I guess," Melissa G. told me at lunch.

"Gee, thanks, Melissa," I said back. I didn't mean to be sarcastic, but I couldn't help it—I still didn't trust her.

"Well, I know what it's like to be on *real* TV,"

she said. "Good thing you didn't cave under the pressure," Melissa said.

"Um, I guess," I replied. I looked over at Sophia sitting next to me, and she just rolled her eyes.

"Anyway, I hope you find the drum," Melissa G. added. "Rachel is a real reporter. A professional. She'll expect a lot. I hope you don't let her down." Then she walked away smiling. Ugh. She makes me so angry sometimes!

"Just ignore her," Sophia said.

"Yeah, you know how she gets when she thinks other people are more famous than her," added Javier, pushing his night-vision goggles up on his head.

"Javier, why are you wearing night-vision goggles during the day?" Lizzie asked him. Shakira and Lizzie were sitting at our lunch table, too.

"Yeah. You look ridiculous!" Shakira said.

"Because," Javier said, "you never know when you might be in a dark closet and need to see something. Also—they look awesome!" And then Javier struck a pose with his hands on his hips like he was in a fashion show.

We all laughed. Shakira shook her head and opened her vanity mirror to check her hair for the hundredth time that day. The mirror sang, "You look faaabulous" for the hundredth time that day! It was starting to get on my nerves.

I reached into my backpack to pull out my lunch box, but I felt something strange. It was a piece of notebook paper in the side pocket. I pulled it out and opened it up. The paper had a message written in pink ink!

"Hey, guys, look!" I cried. "It's an anonymous

note. Just like the one we got about Sophia's costume! Our anonymous source is back!"

I read the note out loud. It said:

Alyssa took the drum home. I saw it in her room!

"What?" asked Sophia. "Alyssa took it home? But why?"

"It really does seem like Alyssa might have been lying about putting the drum in the upstairs closet," said Javier.

"Maybe she stole it!" added Shakira.

"I don't know. But we can't assume anything!" I said. I remembered my *papi* telling me that news reporters have to keep an open mind. That means don't make any assumptions. Just find the facts!

"We have to talk to Alyssa and ask her what really happened, right, Emma?" Javier said, putting his night-vision goggles back over his eyes.

"Yup, yup!" I answered.

"And we should really try to figure out who's been sending these anonymous notes," added Sophia. "How do we know for sure she saw the drum at Alyssa's house? What if the anonymous source is lying?"

"Good point, Sophia!" I said. "We don't know anything for sure yet. We need to find the facts!"

But I still wasn't sure how we were going to get all the facts. As I thought about this, I started playing with my curl again. I pulled it down and it bounced back up like always. As soon as it bounced to my head, an idea popped into my brain again! Just like last time. *That's so strange*, I thought. *It's almost like my curl is magic or something.* I'd have to think about that later. First, I had an idea . . .

"Javier, do you have your magnifying glass with you?" I asked.

"Of course!" Javier said, and rummaged through his spy kit. "Ta-da! Here it is."

"There's something strange on this note, can you take a look?"

"Sure!"

Javier put his night-vision goggles up over his forehead and started inspecting the note with his magnifying glass.

"Hmm. That's interesting," Javier said after a minute.

"What? What is it?" we all asked.

"Well, it looks like the writer of this note . . . likes grape jelly. There's a purple jelly smudge on here."

"So what? Everyone likes jelly," Shakira scolded.

"Okay, okay . . . I know. Wait, there's something else," Javier continued.

"What is it?" I asked.

"Whoever wrote this note also likes hearts. Look, instead of dots, she drew tiny hearts. Here above the letter *i*, and here at the bottom of this exclamation point. And look here at the end of the sentence. A small heart instead of a period."

"Hmm. That's interesting," I said. "So the anonymous source is someone who uses a pink pen, likes to eat grape jelly, and likes to write with hearts."

We all started scanning the lunchroom, wondering who that could be. Who kept sending us anonymous tips? I saw Gabriella walk into the lunchroom.

"Could it be Gabriella?" I said out loud. "She knows about my show, and about our drum investigation. And she knows Alyssa. Maybe she knows what happened?"

"That's possible," said Sophia, "but, Emma, think about it. Remember the anonymous note you got when my lion costume was missing? How would Gabriella have known about that? I don't think it's her."

Sophia was right. It couldn't be Gabriella. She had nothing to do with the missing costume investigation.

Suddenly Geraldine the lunch lady was standing right near us and yelling, "Okay, lunchtime is over. Everybody clean your stuff up, throw your trash in the trash, and get outta here!"

We lined up and went outside to play. There were so many mysteries to solve! I touched my special curl again.

I hope you really are a magic curl. We're gonna need you!

CHAPTER EIGHT

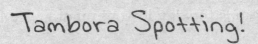

Tambora Spotting!

WE didn't have dance rehearsal after school that day, so we couldn't interview Alyssa yet. Instead I went straight home and did my homework right away so I could think about the case and file another news report. I sat at my desk in my room and wrote in my purple reporter pad,

Clue #4: The anonymous source says
        Alyssa took the drum home.

 67

As soon as Papi got home from work, I told him what happened. He had big news for me, too.

"I spoke to that reporter, Rachel Cheng, on the phone today. She received a phone call from a viewer who says he saw the tambora drum on the M4 bus the day it went missing. He thought it was odd to see a drum sitting on the seat by itself, so he took a picture of it with his cell phone. Rachel sent it to me. Take a look. Is that the drum?"

"That's it!!" I screamed.

"Ow, Emma, not in my ear, please," Papi said.

"Sorry, Papi. But that's the missing drum! See, it has the flower painted on the side next to the flag of the Dominican Republic. We found it!"

"Not so fast," said Papi. "The viewer said he pointed the drum out to the bus driver and then got off at the next stop. He doesn't know what happened to it after that."

"Papi," I said, "I just thought of something. The anonymous source said the drum was at Alyssa's house. How could the drum be on the bus *and* at Alyssa's house?"

"That's a great question," Papi replied.

"I think we need to interview the bus driver. Come on, let's go!" I shouted, running to get my camera phone.

"Hold on a minute, Emma. It's too late now. You have school tomorrow. I'll tell you what: I'll pick you up from dance class after work tomorrow, and I will let you know *if* we are able to find the bus driver and talk to him. No guarantees. Deal?"

"Deal!"

I was getting so excited. I knew we would find the drum! I pulled out my purple reporter pad and wrote:

Clue #5: A viewer saw the drum on the M4 bus!

Then I hurried upstairs to file my next report. I explained everything we learned today.

"Tomorrow we're going to crack this case when we talk to the bus driver! I mean *if* we can find the bus driver and ask him what happened. Keep your fingers crossed! Thanks for watching 'Emma Is On the Air'!"

After school the next day, I met up with every-one at dance class and told them about what happened with Rachel Cheng and the bus driver. We decided to wait till after class to talk to Alyssa.

"There she is, in the corner," Sophia pointed out after class ended. Alyssa was packing up her dance clothes.

"Great," I answered. "Here, Sophia—you take the camera phone. And, Shakira, you can hold the microphone again, if you want to."

"Thanks, Emma!" Shakira grabbed the Emma microphone. Then she pulled out her vanity again to look in the mirror, and we all heard it sing, "You look faaabulous."

"Ugh! Do you have to look in that thing every two seconds?" Javier grumbled.

"Yes, I do!" Shakira insisted as she rolled her eyes at Javier. "Do you have to wear those silly night-vision goggles everywhere we go?"

"Yes, I do!" Javier spat back. "They're important for finding clues! Besides . . . I think they help me dance better. You know . . . when everyone's spinning around, I can see better." Javier spun in place with his goggles on his head.

"You're so weird, Javier," Shakira said.

"Okay, relax, you guys," Sophia chimed in. "Both of your toys are awesome. We have to interview Alyssa before she leaves. Let's go."

We all followed Sophia across the room.

"Hey, Alyssa," I said.

"Hey," she answered. She still sounded sad.

"So, we've made some progress in the case, and we're getting really close to finding the tambora drum."

"What?" she asked, sounding surprised. "But how?"

"Someone called Rachel Cheng and said he saw it sitting in a seat on the M4 bus," Sophia answered.

Alyssa didn't say anything. She looked nervous.

"Also, we interviewed a dancer from the upstairs class who says she never saw you put the drum in the upstairs closet," added Shakira.

"*Also*," Javier said, "we got a note from a witness who said she saw the drum at your house!"

Finally I said, "I have to ask, Alyssa, did you steal the tambora drum?"

Then Alyssa started to cry. We didn't know what to do.

"Emma, it's all my fault!" Alyssa was sniffling.

"It's okay, just talk to us. Tell us what happened," Sophia told her in a calm voice. Sophia was so kind to everyone.

"Okay, here's what really happened," Alyssa began. "The day before Rachel Cheng came to do the story on our dance group, I went to lock the drum up in the closet like I always do after class. But this time the closet was full. There were too many costumes in there. I was in a rush to get home, so I decided to just take the drum with me and bring it back for class the next day. I knew my *tía* wouldn't be happy about that, so I didn't tell her. I figured it would be fine—and it *was* fine. I took the drum home, and nothing went wrong."

Alyssa looked down again, wiping her eyes. She was crying again, we could tell, but she took a deep breath and kept talking.

"The next day after school, I took the M4 bus to dance class. I had the drum on my lap. Then a bunch of my friends got on the bus, and we started talking. I wanted to show them my new cell phone case, and it was in my backpack. So I put the drum down on the seat next to me and got out my backpack to find my phone."

Alyssa paused again and sighed.

"And then you forgot the drum," I finished for her.

"Yes," she answered. "I was so busy talking to my friends, I completely forgot I had the drum with me. I left it on the bus. I was so scared to tell my *tía* the truth, I made up the story about locking it in the upstairs closet. I'm so sorry. I wish I could just get that drum back!"

Suddenly my *papi* walked into the dance studio, interrupting our interview.

"Hi, guys—you ready to go talk to the bus driver?" Papi asked us.

"You found him?" I asked with a hopeful smile.

"You got lucky, kid," Papi answered. "I have a friend who works for the Transit Authority. He's *my* source." Papi winked.

"Alyssa," I said, turning back to her as she wiped away another tear, "come with us. We're going to interview the bus driver and find the drum!"

CHAPTER
NINE

The Man in Uniform

BY now, it was dark outside, and a little bit rainy. We all piled into the car.

"You okay back there?" Papi called to Javier, who was sitting all the way in the back.

"Yup! This is so cool. With my night-vision goggles, I can see everything! Hey, Mr. Perez, did you know there's three pieces of popcorn under the seat back here?"

"Oh. Ah . . . I did not know that. Thanks, Javier."

"You're welcome!" Javier called back. Then he picked the popcorn off the floor and ate it!

"Ew!!!!" Shakira shrieked. We were all pretty disgusted.

"What?" Javier said. "I like popcorn!"

"Now, guys," Papi said trying to get our attention, "My source tells me the driver we want to talk to is a man named Jason. I called ahead, and he was nice enough to agree to talk to us. He even said you guys could interview him on camera."

"Yippee!" I squealed.

"Does he really have the drum?" asked Alyssa.

"We're not quite sure yet," Papi answered as he turned a corner. "He didn't have time to go into detail about what happened. He just said to meet him at the bus depot at six when he gets off his shift. Here we are," Papi said as he drove into the bus parking lot. "Right on time."

We all got out of the car and ran over to a little building in the back of the parking lot. Inside was a small office with a man standing next to a wooden desk and a metal filing cabinet. He had a name tag that said *Jason*. And he was still wearing his blue bus driver uniform. I'd never interviewed someone wearing a uniform before! This was so cool.

"Hello," said Jason. "Welcome to the bus depot. Now how can I help you?"

"Hi," I said back. "We're working on a very important investigation, and we need to do an interview with you."

"Yes, I heard something about that. Not a problem. Should I stand right here?"

"Yes, that's perfect," Sophia replied. She had already gotten the camera phone and microphone out.

I looked over to Sophia and Shakira, and they were ready to go. Javier was inspecting the office with his goggles. Alyssa stood next to Papi, looking worried.

"Thank you again for doing this. We're very grateful," Papi told Jason.

"It's no problem. I trust Nick with my life. Any friend of Nick's is a friend of mine. I hope I can help."

"Nick is my *source*," Papi explained to us.

Oh, I thought. *That's why Papi says that it's important have a source you can trust.*

I turned to Jason and said, "Yeah, thanks, I hope you can help us, too." I looked at Shakira, and she pointed the microphone at Jason.

"Okay, let's get started," I continued. "Jason, can you please tell me what happened on the bus when you found the drum?"

"Sure thing," he answered. "I was driving down my regular route that afternoon. We had just passed 181st Street when a passenger tapped me on the shoulder. He told me a drum had been left on a seat near the back. When we got to the next stop, I got out of my seat to go take a look. I saw what he was talking about. A big brown drum, with a flower on the side, was just sitting there on one of the seats. I knew right away it was a special drum. I play the guitar, and I knew a beautiful instrument like that shouldn't be left alone. So I picked it up and brought it over to the driver's seat for safekeeping. I kept it there by my side until I got back to the bus depot."

"Do you have the drum here?" Alyssa asked hopefully.

"Well, that's the thing," he answered.

"It's in the lost and found, isn't it?" Javier chimed in from across the room.

"Well, that's where I put it," Jason answered.

"Let's go get it!" Shakira shouted.

"I'm afraid there's a problem," Jason continued. "Someone already picked it up. A teenage boy was here yesterday and said the drum belonged to him."

"A teenage boy?" I asked.

"Who? Did he give his name?" Alyssa asked.

"Everyone has to sign the log," answered Jason, nodding. "Let's take a look."

We waited anxiously while Jason the bus driver grabbed a folder from the file cabinet. He took out a piece of paper and started scanning it.

"Ah, there we go," he said, pointing to a name on the list. "Josh Baker. That's who claimed the drum, Josh Baker."

"What????" Shakira screamed. "THE Josh Baker? He was here??"

"Um, I suppose he was," Jason answered, looking up, a bit startled.

Shakira started jumping up and down like a crazy person.

"Doubtful," Sophia said to Shakira with a sigh.

"Yeah, this is not good," I added.

"What's not good?" Papi asked. "What's going on? Who's Josh Baker?"

"Mr. Perez," Shakira answered, still bouncing, "Josh Baker is like the best singer in the world. Like a million girls think he's gorgeous! I can't believe he has our drum!" She was still beaming and clapping her hands with excitement. Sophia, Javier, and I rolled our eyes.

"Shakira, Josh Baker doesn't have our drum," I told her. "Somebody used a fake name." Suddenly she stopped bouncing and looked really sad.

"How do you know it's fake?" she asked.

"Do you really think Josh Baker came to this bus depot yesterday for a drum?" Javier answered.

"It doesn't seem likely," Papi added.

Shakira looked crushed. We were all sad. This meant the drum was gone again, and we had no idea who took it. I was so disappointed I wanted to cry, and Alyssa started to tear up again. Now what? It felt like we were never going to get the drum back.

I had to think of something. So I started playing with my curl again. *C'mon, magic curl, I need an idea!*

I pulled on my curl and made it stretch it all the way down as far as it would go.

"Emma, what are you doing?" Shakira asked. "You're going to mess up your hair!"

"Just a minute," I told her.

After I got my curl to stretch past my waist, I let it go, and it sprang right back up to my head. Then *bam!* It worked! The curl really was magic. I had an idea.

"Jason, can I take a look at the log?"

"Sure," he said as he handed it over to me.

Just as I suspected, you had to write down

more information than just your name. You had to write your address, too.

"Look, he wrote his address down next to his name," I told everyone, "but I can't read it. It looks smudged, and the handwriting is too sloppy."

"Give it over here!" Javier called. "I am an expert at sloppy handwriting! Miss Thompson said my handwriting was some of the sloppiest she's seen!" He pulled out his magnifying glass and focused on the address.

"Hmm . . . this is pretty messy. And smudgy. But I think I got it. It says, 'Washington High School.'"

"Ugh. That's not an address," I sighed, disappointed. Alyssa perked her head up.

"That's my school," she said. "He goes to my school."

CHAPTER
TEN

"Josh Baker"—
Whoever That Is

WHEN we got home that night, I wrote down
the new clues and filed my report.

Clue #6: Alyssa admitted she left
   the drum on the bus and lied
   about it.

Clue #7: Bus driver Jason took the
   drum to the lost and found.

Clue #8: A boy from Washington High
   School took the drum from the

lost and found. He used a fake
name, Josh Baker.

That weekend we spent the whole time rehearsing and thinking. But we were stumped. Why
would someone at Alyssa's school take the
drum? We went back to class the following
week—with no good ideas.

"Emma, I'm starting to get nervous," Shakira
said on the school bus in the morning. "The
parade is in two days, and we have to have
the tambora drum for the full dress rehearsal
tomorrow."

"And," added Sophia, "my mom and I saw
Maestra Soto at the grocery store over the weekend. She seemed so sad. She told my mother
that her grandfather gave her that drum just

before he died. She was supposed to take care of it for him and make sure it didn't sit on a shelf. He wanted it to continue to make beautiful music."

"Wow," I said as I played with my curls. "You're right, we have to find the drum today."

Javier's head popped out of the seat across the aisle from us.

"But how are we supposed to find someone at Washington High? I mean, that's a high school. Those kids are *big*."

"I know, I know . . ." I said.

"Emma, why do you keep touching your curls? You're gonna stretch them out, and then they won't be fabulous anymore!" Shakira warned.

"Okay," I said, making a decision. "I have a secret to tell you guys."

Sophia, Shakira, and Javier all leaned in close to listen.

"I . . . I have a *magic curl.*"

"What? What do you mean a magic curl?" Shakira looked unsure.

"I don't know . . ." said Sophia.

"That's completely awesome!" said Javier.

"No, really, I do." I told them about all the times my bouncing curl helped me before. "Watch . . . it really does work." I took my curl and pulled it all the way down again. As far as it would stretch. And then I let it bounce back up. Everyone looked at me waiting for the magic to happen. I was waiting, too. At first nothing did happen. Then—*bam!* Another great idea!

"AHA!" I shouted. They all jumped in their seats!

"What?" asked Sophia.

"I know what to do!"

"What is it?" asked Shakira.

"We have to figure out who else was on the bus with Alyssa! Her group of friends were there, right? Maybe one of them saw something!"

"Good idea. Because 'Josh Baker,'" Sophia said, making air quotes with her hands, "whoever that really is, must have seen it on the bus that day, too. How else would he know to go get it from the bus depot?"

"Exactly," I said. "Maybe one of her other friends saw 'Josh Baker' on the bus." I used air quotes, too, and we all giggled a little.

"Yeah, 'Josh Baker,'" Javier added, making the air quotes again. "I bet 'Josh Baker' looks like an alien." He started laughing.

"Um, what are you talking about?" Shakira asked with disdain.

"What?" Javier answered. "Sophia's the one who called him an alien. And Emma gave him the alien ears, too," Javier explained, using the air quotes again.

"Javier, those aren't alien ears. They're called air quotes. See, my fingers are making the shape of quotation marks," Sophia said, demonstrating the air quotes again.

"Oh. Right." Javier looked embarrassed. "Whatever. Hey, Emma, can I see your magic curl?"

"Um, I guess," I replied as I leaned over to him.

Javier held the end of my curl up to his head and started pulling at it.

"Ouch!" I yelled.

"Sorry . . . I was hoping your curl could teach my curls a thing or two!"

*   *   *

"Okay, boys and girls," Maestra Soto said, speaking to all the mangulina dancers later that afternoon. "This is our last class before the final dress rehearsal tomorrow. I want you to give it your all."

"But what about the drum? Have we found it yet?" asked another dancer.

"No, not yet," answered Maestra. "But let me worry about that. You focus on your twirls."

We all got in our places for rehearsal, and the music began. Maestra pulled me aside.

"Emma, how's your investigation going? I miss that tambora drum so much. I can't imagine performing in the parade without it," she said with a sad face.

"Don't worry, Maestra," I told her. "We have a plan! We'll find that tambora drum—I promise! There's no way they can kick us out of the parade!"

"Thank you, Emma. You've been wonderful. *¡Una niña buenísima!* Wait . . . kick us out of the parade? What do you mean?" she called after me. But I spotted Alyssa on the other side of the dance studio.

"Sorry, Maestra, I have to go get another clue. Talk later!"

I twirled over to Alyssa across the dance floor.

"Alyssa," I said, "I need to ask you something before we rehearse."

"Sure, what is it?"

"I need to know who was on the bus with you the day you left the drum."

"Hmm," Alyssa said. She started thinking. "Well, Laylani was sitting to my left and Monique was next her. Oh, and Marco and his friends were sitting in the back corner."

"Marco? Do you think he's the real 'Josh Baker'? Do you think he might have taken the drum?" I asked.

"No, he would never. Plus he got off the bus before I did. He didn't even know I left it there. But his friends were still on the bus."

"Which friends?"

"I don't know. I've never really hung out with those boys before. I don't know their names."

"Great. Now what?" I asked. I was starting to get worried. "We have to find those kids. One of them has the drum."

"I have an idea," Alyssa said with cautious

excitement. "If we can't find the kid who took the drum, maybe we can convince him to find *us*?"

What was Alyssa talking about? How could we make a high school kid find us?

CHAPTER
ELEVEN

High School

THE next morning, I took extra care getting ready for school. The final dress rehearsal was supposed to happen that evening. I decided to put my hair up rehearsal-style in the morning, because we had big plans to finally get the drum back after school. So I pulled my hair back in a tight bun and tied special red, white, and blue ribbons around it. I looked in the mirror and smiled.

Alyssa really did come up with a great idea to find the drum. Last night, she made dozens of flyers offering a reward for anyone who could return the drum to us. The flyers said: LOST DRUM and underneath  was a picture of the tambora. Then: *Please return anonymously—no questions asked—to locker 53 after school today at 3:30. There is a $50 reward for the safe return of the drum. If the drum is returned later than 3:30, there will be no reward.*

Alyssa said locker 53 was empty so we could use it to lure the drum thief. She was using her own babysitting money for the reward. I said he didn't deserve a reward, but she insisted. Alyssa still blamed herself for what happened.

The plan was for Alyssa to pick us all up from school today. We told our parents she was taking us to dance class. And technically she was. But first we made a stop at Washington High School. I started getting nervous as we walked up to the school.

"Come on, guys, this way," said Alyssa as she opened a side door to the high school. I had never been to a high school before. It was a lot bigger than my school. And a little scary.

"Um, Emma, are you sure this is a good idea?" asked Javier as a boy with a mustache walked by us. Javier looked nervous, too.

"Yeah, maybe we should just let Alyssa get the drum back without us," added Sophia as a girl with bright red lipstick walked up the stairs.

"But, guys," I reminded them, "we have to confront the drum thief as soon as we find him. We have to ask him why he took the drum. Our viewers need to know what happened!"

"That's right," Shakira chimed in. "Don't be scared. It's just high school. My big sister goes here, too. I promise it's not that bad." Shakira pulled out her compact mirror to check her hair and make sure it looked good enough for high school. Then we all heard the mirror again sing, "You look faaabulous."

"Ugh!" groaned Javier. "Not that again! You're gonna embarrass us in high school!"

"Fine, fine. I'm putting it away. Relax."

"Everybody needs to relax," said Alyssa. "It's almost three thirty. We have to go wait by locker 53."

We headed upstairs and found the locker.

It was 3:20. In ten minutes, the drum thief would be there. We decided the hide around the corner from the locker so the drum thief wouldn't see us and run away. Sophia got out the camera phone, and I got my microphone ready to go.

"But, Emma," said Sophia, "if we hide around the corner, how will we see what's happening? How will we know when the drum thief arrives and when we should start recording?"

"Oh. Um. Good point. I don't know," I answered. This was tough.

"What if I peek from a classroom across the hall," offered Javier. "When I see the drum thief arrive, I can use my walkie-talkie to tell you guys to start recording?"

"Great idea!" I said.

Javier grabbed the walkie-talkies from his spy kit.

"Oh, no," he said as he started playing with them. "They're not working." Javier pulled the battery covers off. Empty. The walkie-talkies needed batteries. And we didn't have any.

"Sorry. I haven't used these yet. I didn't know they needed juice."

"That's okay," I said, trying not to panic. "We just need a new plan. I have to think. I need my magic curl!"

I reached for my magic curl, but it wasn't there. Uh-oh.

"Emma, your curl is pulled back in your bun," Shakira pointed out.

"I know!" I said. "Now what are we gonna do? I need that curl! We need an idea, and I can't come up with one without my curl. I just can't!"

"Emma, calm down," said Sophia.

"I can't calm down! The drum thief will be here in . . ." I looked at the clock. It said 3:24. "Six minutes. He'll be here in six minutes! We need a plan. I can't let the viewers down. We need to show them who the thief is! I need my magic curl!"

"Emma," Sophia said, "think about it. You've come up with plenty of ideas before you thought that curl was magic. It was great and has helped a lot, but you don't *need* it. You can do it on your own. I know you can."

But I wasn't sure if I could. I looked at the clock. 3:26. I needed a plan! But I couldn't think. I looked over toward Shakira. She didn't seem worried at all. She was just fixing her hair again. How could she fix her hair at a time like this?

Then—*boom*. It came to me. Even without my magic curl, I knew just what to do.

I ran over to Shakira as fast as I could and grabbed the pink singing vanity mirror out of her hands.

"Hey!" she shouted. "Emma, what are you doing with my mirror? I need that!"

"Actually, *we* need it," I called back—I was already running toward locker 53. "Just for a few minutes," I told her. I didn't have time to explain. I ran over to the locker, opened it up and took out the envelope Alyssa had put there with the reward money. I replaced it with the mirror instead.

Then I grabbed my reporter pad and wrote a quick note that said, *Open the vanity mirror. Your reward money is inside.*

I placed the note on top of the mirror and ran back over to the group hiding around the corner. I looked at the clock. It said 3:30. I put my finger over my mouth to tell everyone to shush. It was time to catch our thief!

CHAPTER TWELVE

"You Look Faaabulous!"

WE were all huddled around the corner and couldn't see a thing. But we could hear. We heard footsteps walking toward us. Then they stopped. Then we heard a squeaking noise that sounded like it might be coming from a locker door.

Sophia looked at me like she was ready to start recording. I shook my head and held up a finger, telling her to wait one more minute.

Then it happened. We all heard it . . .

"You look faaabulous!" screeched from Shakira's vanity mirror.

"Now, Sophia!" I said to her. "Let's go!"

Sophia pressed record, and we ran around the corner over to locker 53. Alyssa gasped.

"David?" she said in shock. "*David?* What are you doing?"

We couldn't believe it. It was David Soto—Maestra Soto's son! He was standing there with the drum in his hand as the vanity mirror sang over and over, "You look faaabulous!"

"I ... uh ... um ... here, this is for you," he said as he handed the drum to Alyssa. She grabbed it and set it down on the floor away from him.

"But, David, why do *you* have the drum?"

"You took the drum from the lost and found at the bus depot. Didn't you?" I said as I

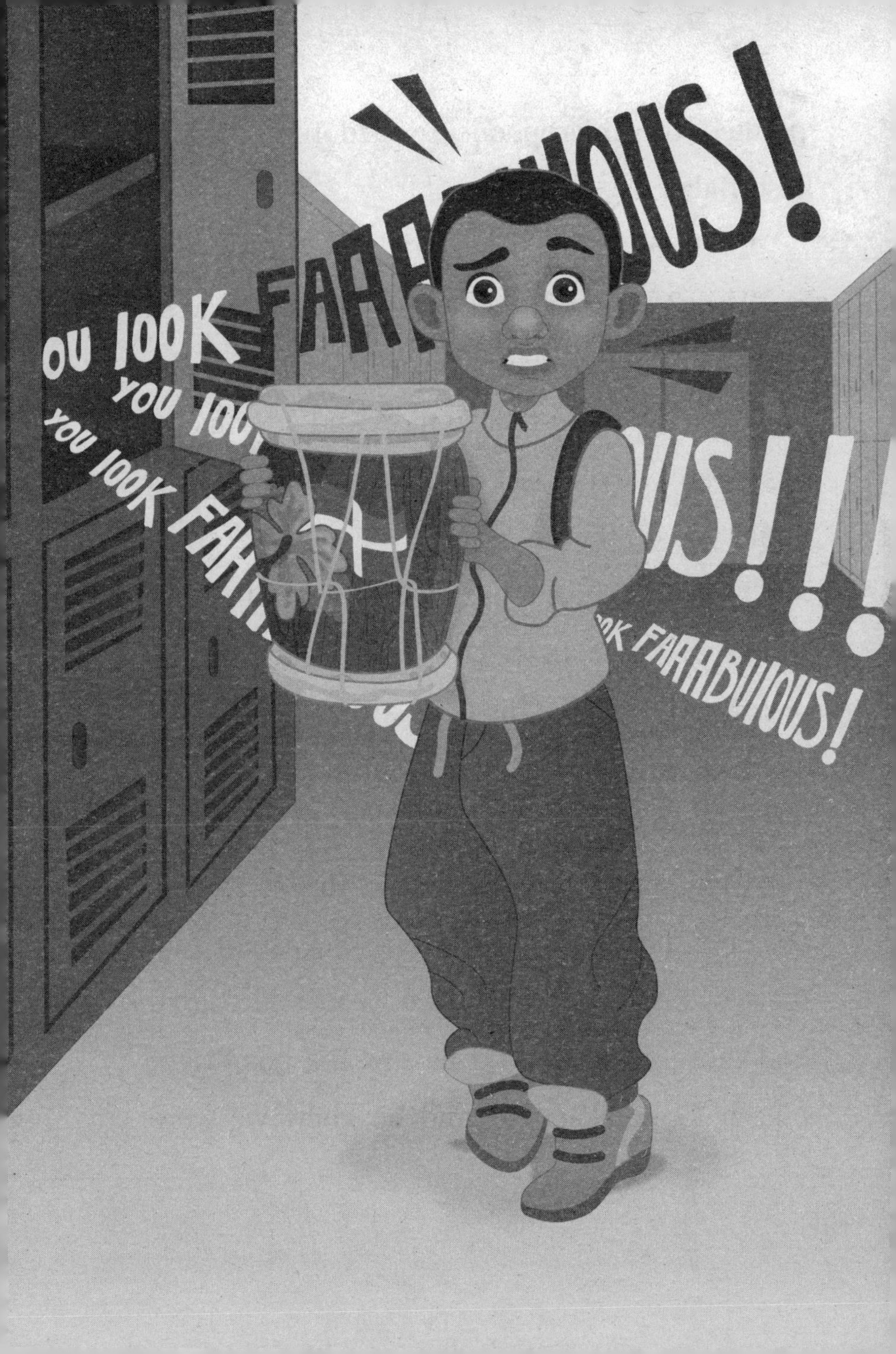
FARR
UOUS!
OU LOOK
YOU LOO
YOU LOOK FAH
OUS!!!
OK FARRABUIOUS!

pointed the microphone toward him. "You're Josh Baker."

"Well. Okay, fine. Yes, I did!" David answered.

"Why? Why did you do it?" shouted Alyssa with tears in her eyes. "You're my own cousin. How could you do that to me? And your mother's been worried sick about that drum! How could you do that to *her*?"

"I meant to give it back to her. Honest . . . but things got complicated." David looked at the ceiling. And then at his feet.

"Can you please explain?" I asked him. "From the beginning?"

"Okay, fine," David began. "Alyssa, I knew you left the drum on the bus. Sebastian told me—you know the kid who hangs out with Marco and those guys. He said he saw the bus driver take it for safekeeping, and he knew we were cousins, so he told me what happened. I figured it was probably at the lost and found at the bus depot, so I went to go pick it up."

"Okay," I said. "Sounds good. But why didn't you just give it to her? We've been going crazy looking for it. We almost missed the Thanksgiving Day Parade!"

"Well, that's it. I wanted to miss the parade! And I realized this could be my chance. Maybe if you didn't find the drum in time, we could all just skip that dumb parade. So I gave a fake name at the bus depot. Josh Baker . . . I hate that guy. I figured no one would know it was me. And I hid the drum at home."

"What? You *wanted* to miss the parade?" Shakira asked.

"Why?" asked Javier. "Why would you want to miss being in the Thanksgiving Day Parade??"

"Number one, it's embarrassing," answered David. "I'm tired of doing the mangulina. Number two, Mom has been so busy rehearsing for the parade she stopped coming to my soccer games. She didn't even realize we made the play-offs! Number three, she wouldn't give me the money to go to our championship game in Boston. She said I didn't deserve it because I got a D on my history test and I had a bad attitude. Whatever. I was mad at her. I figured, if I can't go to my soccer tournament, then she can't be in the parade."

"David!" Alyssa said in shock. "How could you do that to your mother? And to our great-grandfather?"

"I know. I didn't really know the whole story about great-grandfather giving her that drum. I started to feel bad. I guess I did have a bad attitude. I was going to give it back, I just didn't know how. Then I saw your flyer and figured I could give it back without getting caught. Plus I could use the fifty bucks to go to my soccer tournament. I didn't know your little friends were gonna put me on the news!" David said, pointing to me and Sophia and Shakira and Javier.

"David, you're not on just *any* news show," I told him. "You're on 'Emma Is On the Air'! And you shouldn't have done that to your mother."

"Yeah," Javier agreed, "you should've just told your mom how you feel instead of lying."

"Okay, kid. You're right. And I'm sorry. I'm glad this is over and you have your drum back."

"This is *not* over! Wait till I tell Tía what happened!" said Alyssa. She and David started arguing.

"That's right!" I said. "Maestra Soto doesn't know we have the drum back yet. The dress rehearsal is going to start soon."

"We better call her before she tells the parade organizers the drum is gone," added Sophia.

"Better yet," I shouted, "let's show her!" I started running down the hall toward the exit. Everyone followed.

CHAPTER
THIRTEEN

"¡Fabuloso!"

WE hurried out of Washington High School and ran down the block to my house to file our news report. This time, everyone told part of the story: me, Sophia, Javier, and Shakira. Then we posted it.

Later at the dress rehearsal, Maestra Soto gave me a huge hug!

"*¡Ay, gracias, mi amor!* Thank you again, Emma! My love! You are a lifesaver. I saw your news report. I know my *abuelo* in heaven will be pleased to see his drum in the parade! And David and I had a nice long talk. He's in big trouble, but we were also honest with each other about what's been going on the last few weeks. He apologized. And I did, too."

"I'm glad to hear that," I replied. "I'm so glad the drum is back. Now we're going to be able to perform! I was really worried we were going to get kicked out!"

"Yes, you mentioned that before. But we were never going to get kicked out of the parade."

"We weren't? I thought without the drum, the parade organizers wouldn't want us anymore."

"No, honey. I told the parade organizers what happened. I was worried they would be disappointed, but they said they were happy to have us. They loved the drum, but we were going to perform either way."

"Oh. Oops." I felt a little embarrassed.

"Well, now that we *do* have the drum we know for sure our performance will be *espectacular*!" I said.

"Yes, we will be spectacular!" Maestra agreed.

And we were. The next day at the parade, we danced down the whole parade route with our skirts twirling high in the air. So many people were cheering for us! Even Javier managed to spin twice in a row without hitting the ground.

Rachel Cheng the reporter was there, too— and she interviewed me again for the real news! After we finished our Thanksgiving dinner at home that night, we sat down to watch the news.

"You might remember, Las Palomas was missing a rare and beautiful drum that was supposed to be an integral part of their performance," Rachel said in her report on TV. "It's called a tambora drum. But in the end, they found it, thanks to this dancer, Emma Perez. She's an ace reporter herself, and she has a team of junior journalists working with her." Then Rachel showed all of us: me, Sophia, Javier, and Shakira. "Together they tracked down the drum in the nick of time!"

Then I saw myself on TV saying, "We just had to follow the clues and never give up. Sometimes the solution is right there in your head already. You just have to be brave and let your brain do the work!"

After the news story ended, Mom said, "Emma, I can't tell you how proud I am of you."

My baby sister, Mia, giggled and said in her baby voice, "Em-mama!"

"Mia's right, *mi amor*," said Papi. "That was a great job! You gave a fabulous answer to Rachel in her news report! *¡Fabuloso!*"

"Papi—please can you use another word?! If I hear the word *faaabulous* one more time I'm gonna go nuts!"

We all started laughing. I was pretty proud of myself, too. I'm still not sure how I came up with the idea to put Shakira's vanity mirror in the locker. It just popped into my head—even though my magic curl was trapped in my bun. I guess my brain has its own magic!

Good thing, too, because that mirror helped us out big-time. Even Javier admitted it turned out to be a pretty cool detective tool. I think Javier and Shakira both realized that even though they are different kinds of people who like different kinds of things, that doesn't mean they can't be friends. Javier promised not to bother Shakira about her mirror anymore. And Shakira even agreed to try out Javier's night-vision goggles!

"Oh, Emma, I almost forgot," said Mom. "This came for you yesterday."

"What is it?" I asked.

"I'm not sure. Someone slipped this envelope under our door."

I took a look at it. The envelope said *Emma Is On the Air* and it was written in . . . pink ink. The anonymous source! But how did she know where I lived? I nervously opened the envelope. Inside was another anonymous note! It had only five words, written in pink.

Emma, I need your help . . .

EMMA'S TIPS FOR NOT-BORING NEWS

1. Make friends with a real reporter!
Real reporters are awesome.
They wear brightly colored coats
and know <u>lots</u> about the news.
Sometimes they will even show you
their real microphones and cameras
if you ask nicely. Maybe your
teacher can invite a reporter
to school for career day!

2. **Turn toys into tools!** You never
know when a bag of wooden blocks,
a baby-doll stroller, or even a silly

makeup mirror can help you crack
a case or break a news story. Be
creative!

3. **Your brain has magic!** Sometimes
it might feel like other people's
brains work better than yours.
It's not true! All brains are like
magic. You just have to think hard,
and the ideas will pop right out!

4. **Have all kinds of friends!** When
your friends like different kinds
of things, you'll never be bored!
And you'll always have cool news
stories. That's because everyone
will think of something unique!

Emma will be back ON THE AIR in

#4: UNDERCOVER!